For Sharon Cantor
K. L.

In memory of
EVERETT HAFNER,
*my favourite
science fair bunny*
M. H.

First published 2000 by Walker Books Ltd
87 Vauxhall Walk, London SE11 5HJ

10 9 8 7 6 5 4 3 2 1

Text © 2000 Kathryn Lasky
Illustrations © 2000 Marylin Hafner

This book has been typeset in Sabon.

Printed in Hong Kong

British Library Cataloguing in Publication Data
A catalogue record for this book is
available from the British Library.

ISBN 0-7445-5665-1

SCIENCE FAIR BUNNIES

BY KATHRYN LASKY

ILLUSTRATED BY MARYLIN HAFNER

WALKER BOOKS
AND SUBSIDIARIES
LONDON • BOSTON • SYDNEY

CLYDE WOKE UP AND GROANED.

"Oh, no! My bean plants have wilted!"

"Not wilted, Clyde," his older brother Jefferson said. "They croaked. Dead. Dead, dead, dead."

"But they were for my Science Fair project," Clyde moaned. "I grew them from beans."

"I'd say you're in big trouble," said Jefferson. "Up a creek without a paddle."

Clyde went to call his best friend.
"Rosemary?" he said. "I've got bad news. My bean plants ... they ... died."

"Mine, too," said Rosemary. "What are we going to do? The Science Fair is only a week away."
"I know," Clyde sighed.

"Why so glum?" Clyde's mother asked at breakfast.
"My Science Fair project ... it's ..." Clyde hesitated.
"Kaput," said Jefferson.
"Oh, dear. Well, I'm sure you'll think of something,
Clyde. You're so clever," his mother said.

"Give me a break," muttered Jefferson.

Clyde did not feel at all clever.

"You want to see clever?" Jefferson said. He got up and came back with a battery box, two wires, and a pickle. "Buster and I are illuminating pickles. Pickle juice is salty and it works like battery juice." Jefferson stuck a wire in each end of the pickle and connected the wires to the battery.

"Ta da!" he exclaimed. The pickle glowed magnificently.

Clyde grew glummer and glummer.

"Eat your breakfast, Clyde," said his mother.

Clyde bit into his bagel. "Ouch! I forgot. I have a loose tooth."

"Is it ready to come out yet?" his father asked.

"No!" Clyde exclaimed.

He went to look at his new tooth. This was only the second tooth he had ever lost. The first had bled a little but at least the Tooth Fairy had come.

He remembered how he'd wrapped the tooth in a piece of tissue all nice and lumpy and put it under his pillow with a note for the Tooth Fairy, and in the morning there was a shiny coin in its place.

Clyde pushed his tongue against the loose tooth. It moved a little.

Clyde pushed on his tooth all the way to school.
"What have you got in your mouth?" Rosemary
asked in science class.
"A loose tooth."

"Me, too," said Rosemary. "My first."

"Me, too," said Felix, as he and Betty set up a racetrack for their Wheels and Ways project with toy cars. "It's my third."

"My fourth," said Ralph, who was working on a weather chart with Abby. They had recorded the rainfall for the last thirty days. Clyde wished he and Rosemary had thought of a weather project. Weather was so dependable. It happened no matter what.

At dinner that night, Clyde's father said, "Let me look at that tooth."

"Promise not to pull it?" asked Clyde.

"I just want to see it," his father said. He looked into Clyde's mouth. "It's hanging by a thread."

"It's so glistening white," said his mother. "Like a little pearl."

Clyde thought of Granny McBunn. Her teeth were brown. His mother said it came from drinking so much tea.

Suddenly Clyde had an idea. "If I put my tooth in a jar of tea for a week, would it turn the colour of Granny McBunn's?"

"Probably," said Clyde's father.

"Oh, Clyde, what a wonderful experiment! You're so clever!" said his mother.

"Give me a break!" groaned Jefferson.

"But what about the Tooth Fairy?" asked Clyde.

"Well, Clyde," said Jefferson, "is it science or the Tooth Fairy?"

"Would it bleed if you pulled it, Dad?" asked Clyde.

"No," said Clyde's father. "Just one quick tweak."

"OK, Dad. Pull it."

Clyde's mother poured hot water into a jar. Clyde put in a tea bag. He dropped in his tooth and went to the telephone.

"Rosemary, how's your tooth?"

"Hanging by a thread," she said.

Then Clyde told Rosemary what he'd done. His tooth was in tea and she could put hers in orange jelly.

"It's a really good experiment," he said.

"But what about the Tooth Fairy?" Rosemary asked.

"I don't know."

"I've got to think about this, Clyde. It's my first tooth, after all," said Rosemary.

That night, when Clyde's mother tucked him in, she told him again how clever he was.

"That's the third time," Jefferson muttered.

When Clyde fell asleep he had a dream about the Tooth Fairy. He was in a laboratory. There were jars and jars of teeth in different liquids – tea, milk, orange juice, blackcurrant drink, lemonade, cola – all turning strange colours. The Tooth Fairy was wandering around, looking confused. "I just don't understand, Clyde. How could you do this to me?"

"Science," said Clyde. "We did it for science."

He was about to explain how the beans had died when his mother woke him up for school. "Look, Clyde, your tooth is darker!"

Clyde blinked. The tooth *did* look different!

He got out his paper and coloured pencils and drew a picture and labelled it. Mr Bunson, his science teacher, said that record keeping was part of good science. He called it "data".

On his way to school, Clyde wondered what Rosemary had decided. A one-tooth experiment wasn't much. He needed a second tooth at least. He ran his tongue around his mouth. Nothing was loose. Clyde began to despair.

When he got to school Rosemary rushed up to him. "Strawberry!" she cried.

"Strawberry what?" asked Clyde.

"We only had strawberry jelly." Rosemary smiled. There was a big gap where the tooth had been.

"Rosemary! You did it!"

"It was for science, Clyde. Now we need more teeth."

They put up a sign and waited for people to give them teeth. Finally Claudia and Daphne came by.

"Daphne and I lost our teeth this morning," Claudia said. "You can have Daphne's. The Tooth Fairy will give us double the money. It works that way when you're twins."

"That's great!" said Rosemary.

Blackcurrant drink! Clyde thought. *We'll put Daphne's tooth in blackcurrant drink.*

All week long Rosemary and Clyde left the three teeth to soak. Every day they made notes and drew pictures as the teeth in the jars darkened. On the day of the Science Fair, Rosemary's father drove them to school with their posters and a box containing the three jars of teeth.

"Good luck!" Clyde's mother called.

The Science Fair
projects were set up
in the main hall.
Albert had done an
experiment with
bacteria that ate
oil slicks.

Harry and Edward
had done one called
Potions and Explosions,
with baking soda and
vinegar.

"Wow, Rosemary!"
exclaimed Clyde. "Look
at that bacteria experiment!"
Rosemary made a face.
"His parents did it. You can tell."
"Well, I guess no one
could say that about ours."
Clyde sighed.

The judges were coming. "My goodness," said
one judge, "you made a sign asking your classmates
to donate their loose teeth and only one did?"

"Yes," Rosemary nodded.

"It was the Tooth Fairy," explained Clyde.
"They didn't want to disappoint the Tooth Fairy."

"See, we wrote it right there."

"Yes, I see," said another judge. "Very interesting."

The judges made notes and then moved on.

Clyde and Rosemary waited nervously.

Soon it was time for the announcement of the Science Fair awards.

"The award for best presentation of facts goes to Felix and Betty for their Wheels and Ways Experiment," said the head teacher. Everyone clapped.

"The blue ribbon for best scientific procedure goes to Susan, Phoebe and Mark for their Kitchen Crystals Experiment comparing the abilities of sugar-based mixtures to form crystals."
More clapping.

"And finally the blue ribbon for the project that demonstrates the most original and independent work in the entire Science Fair goes to Clyde and Rosemary for their Yucky Teeth Experiment."

"I can't believe it! We did it! We did it!" yelled Rosemary and Clyde, jumping up and down.

"You thought of the idea, Clyde."

"Well, it was just that my tooth was loose. And you gave up your very *first* tooth, Rosemary."

"It was for science," she said.

"I guess so," said Clyde. "I hope the Tooth Fairy understands."

The next morning when Clyde woke up he felt something under his pillow.

It was a nice, lumpy little parcel.

He unwrapped the tissue. A shiny coin glittered, and beside it there was a tea-coloured tooth.

There was a note, too.

Dear Clyde,
Here's your money and here is your tooth.
When it's for Science, you can keep both.
You're so Clever!
Love,
The Tooth Fairy

"Hey!" said Jefferson. "Come and look at my new pickle torch. Want me to wire up that tooth for you and make it glow?"

"No thanks. I think I'll just keep it the way it is."

"For science?" Jefferson asked.

"No, just to remember."

And then Clyde went to call Rosemary
to make sure that she kept her tooth, too –

just to remember.